# The BUTTERCUP F Rainy Day

**Chris Callery made up the story**
**Mary Hoffman wrote the words**
**Margaret Chamberlain drew the pictures**

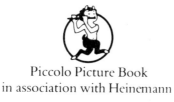

Piccolo Picture Book
in association with Heinemann

First published 1982 by William Heinemann Ltd
This Piccolo edition published 1983 by Pan Books Ltd,
Cavaye Place, London SW10 9PG
in association with William Heinemann Ltd
Text © Callery Productions Ltd and Mary M. Hoffman 1982
Illustrations © Margaret Chamberlain 1982
ISBN 0 330 28076 7
Printed in Spain by
Graficas Reunidas SA, Madrid

Meet the Buttercup Buskers. Here they are,
hard at work with their friend Snowy.

The buskers don't work in an office or factory.
Their job is making people happy. Whenever they
perform their tricks in towns and at fairs,
there are always children watching them.

The buskers spend the summer bowling along
country lanes in their gaily-painted cart.
At night they camp around Snowy's tent.
It's a fine, free life on the open road.

But the sun doesn't always shine, even in summer.
One rainy day, they were hurrying along trying
to find somewhere dry to spend the night.

Snowy pedalled as hard as he could. The wet
animals were clucking and barking and quacking
with excitement, when suddenly. . .

with a slither and a crash, the cart skidded
into a muddy ditch. Snowy had forgotten to put
the brakes on! What was he to do?

Snowy pulled while Billy pushed and butted,
but the cart was stuck fast.

Chip and Snowy went to find help, leaving
the other buskers to guard the cart.

They hadn't gone far when they met a kind farmer
who said Doughnut, his donkey, would help them.

Doughnut was much stronger than Snowy. With
a heave, he pulled the cart out of the mud.

When the buskers took Doughnut back, the farmer
said they could spend the night in his barn.

Mother pig and her piglets were very excited
at having real show business people to stay.

Snowy had the buskers' supper in a picnic
basket. Lettuce for the rabbits, corn for Sergeant
Rooster and his wives, fishheads for the cats.
There was a chocolate cake too, but Snowy
put it back in the basket for the next day.

After supper, the buskers and the pigs settled down to sleep in the warm straw.

Early next morning Sergeant Rooster was out in the farmyard, helping to wake everyone up.

Mother pig took her piglets to find breakfast.

Snowy thanked the farmer for his kindness

and Doughnut for his help

and mother pig for sharing her barn with them.

But mother pig was too worried to say goodbye
to the buskers. She had lost one of her piglets
and was looking for him everywhere.

So the Buttercup Buskers were back on the road.
The sun was shining and the birds were singing.
But that squeaking was spoiling everything.

Snowy got down and oiled the wheels.

But it didn't do the trick. As soon as they
were on their way, the squeaking started again.

It seemed to be coming from the front of the cart.

Snowy opened it. He had found the squeak!
A fat piglet sat in the empty picnic basket,
covered in chocolate cake crumbs.

The buskers gathered round the guilty piglet.
"I was looking forward to that cake," said

Spike the hedgehog, glumly nibbling a crumb.
They took the piglet back to his worried mother.

Then they were off again to the next town. The cart, lighter by one piglet and one cake, bowled merrily along the lane, taking the Buttercup Buskers to their next adventure.